Little James' Big Adventures

Japan!
Janine Iannelli

Illustrated by: Michelle Iannelli

Xlibris
1-888-795-4274
www.Xlibris.com
Orders@Xlibris.com

ISBN: 978-1-6641-7530-3 (sc)
ISBN: 978-1-6641-7531-0 (hc)
ISBN: 978-1-6641-7529-7 (e)

Print information available on the last page

Rev. date: 05/20/2021

This book is dedicated to my beautiful friend Sarah Russo. Thank you for always supporting me and believing in me and my goals. I love you.

Little James dreams of places far far away,

That he hopes to visit and see one day.

Most people take planes or even a boat,

But this little boy travels differently than most.

It's kind of a secret so shhh don't tell,
But Santa Clause made it with a magic Christmas spell!

The adventure begins after mom and dad turn off their light.
Then Susie sits up and asks, "Where are we going tonight?"

James thinks for a moment and then says, "I know!"
He puts their hands on the globe and says, "To Japan we go!"

The walls start to rumble and the ground opens wide,
James and Susie hold hands and get ready for the ride!

"Wheeeeeee!!!!!!"

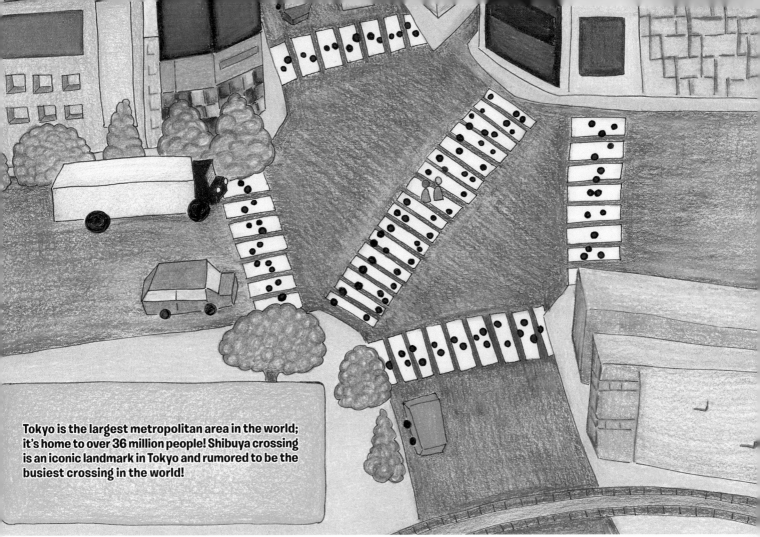

Tokyo is the largest metropolitan area in the world; it's home to over 36 million people! Shibuya crossing is an iconic landmark in Tokyo and rumored to be the busiest crossing in the world!

And suddenly it's still yet noisy and bustling,
And there they are standing in a big city crossing!

"Woah James it's so busy, there are people everywhere!"
They both take a second to stand around and stare.

"What a big intersection we're standing in!"
"That means we're in Tokyo!" James says with a grin.

Sensoji is a Buddhist temple that was originally built to honor and house a golden statue of the goddess Kannon.

"We should get started," says James, "to make the most of our time." They head to the Sensoji temple and then explore the Meiji shrine.

Meiji shrine was built in dedication to Emperor Meiji and Empress Shoken in 1920.

"Next can we see the cherry blossoms?" Susie wants to know.

"Here they call them Sakura," says James, "and of course we can go."

The cherry blossom is the national symbol of Japan. In April, the trees flower for two weeks, this period is known as Hanami which means "flower viewing."

Tokyo tower is 333 meters (1,092 ft) high and was modeled after the Eiffel Tower. It is a communications and observation tower.

Susie skips through the sakura and exclaims, "I love this city! It has so much history and it's super clean and pretty!"

"I agree," says James, as they admire the pretty pink flower, "But I think it's time we move along and see the Tokyo Tower!"

They are standing at the top overlooking the city of Tokyo,
"What an amazing city," says James, "and now let's see Kyoto!"

They place their hands on the globe and just like that they arrive,
They are immediately amazed as they open up their eyes!

Geisha are highly valued entertainers and are well educated in Japanese arts. It takes years of education and training to become a Geisha.

Kimono translates as, "something to wear." It is a traditional Japanese garment and the national dress of Japan.

It's old and historic yet beautiful and calm,
And both James and Susie are silenced by its charm.
They admire the wooden storefronts, and see a Geisha walking by,
"She's perfect, like a doll," says Susie, "Oh my, oh my, oh my!
And their clothing is so beautiful I want to shop where they go!"
"Actually," James says, "her outfit is called a Kimono."

Everyone's very polite and greets, 'Konnichiwa," with a bow.
"That means hello," James informs, "hey what should we do now?"

"Well James," says Susie, "what about a tour?"
"Ooo good idea," James agrees, "there's so much to explore!"

Temples are places of worship in Japanese Buddhism.

Tenruji Temple has been reconstructed since its founding in 1339 due to eight major fires!

They start at Tenruji temple, there is so much to see,
They admire the many structures, ponds, flowers, and trees.

In Japanese tradition, bamboo is a symbol of strength. It actually has a higher tensile strength than steel!

Bamboo is the fastest growing plant in the world! It can grow 3 feet (1 meter) of height in 24 hours in the right climate. Bamboo also releases 30% more oxygen into the atmosphere compared to other plants.

They walk through the bamboo forest and
learn about the strength of the trees,

The stalks are tall and thin and sway gently with the breeze.

"I'm getting hungry," says Susie, "hmm what should we eat?"

"You should try the Ramen," says the tour
guide, "in Japan it can't be beat!"

In Japan, shoes are always removed before entering someone's home and also practiced in some restaurants. Slippers specifically for the indoors are worn throughout the house except for the bathroom where a separate pair of slippers is worn.

They go to try some Ramen, but before they can enter the shop,
They are asked to remove their shoes so they do so on the spot.

"Our mom would love it here!" Susie proclaims,
"She likes us to remove our shoes especially when it rains."

They sit down and are given warm, wet towels for their hands,

"I like this practice," Susie says, "It's great seeing other lands."

Making noise while eating is seen as a lack of manners in Japan however, slurping noodles is the exception. One of the reasons being that slurping noodles allows for more flavor to be tasted.

"Me too," smiles James, as they wait for their ramen to arrive,
Then the server brings it over, and they both give it a try.

"Woah this is delicious!" says Susie, as she slurps the noodles loudly,
"And slurping ramen is customary so we can do it proudly."

Sushi originated as a means of preservation when fermented rice was used to store and preserve fish for an extended period of time. The fish was also heavily salted to prevent the growth of bacteria.

"Now let's have some sushi before we have to go."
"Sure Susie," James answers, "but there
is something you must know,
Sushi is different here, but I think you'll like it better,
It's simpler and lighter and so much fresher!"

The sushi arrives and Susie gives it a try.
Her eyes light up and she says, "I'm not going to lie,
It is a lot different than what I've had before,
But this is so good I need to have some more!"

"Gochiso sama desu," James says to the waiter as they walk away,
"That means *thank you for the meal,* now off to Nara I say!"

There are around 1400 wild deer living in Nara park. Though they are wild they are tame and are protected as Natural monuments in Nara.

They land in Nara park, Susie cheers, "We're here, we're here!"
Then they have a look around and see all the deer!

"James this is amazing! These deer are so friendly and sweet."
They pet the deer and walk the park and feed them a little treat.

They stroll through the city and watch a mochi pounding show,
They both watch intently as two men hammer the dough.

"Is this dessert?" Susie asks, "If so I want to try some."
"It is dessert," James answers, "and we're
definitely going to have some!"

Mochi is a traditional food for the Japanese New Year.

The men yell and shout as they hammer the dough till its done.
Susie giggles in excitement, "I'm having so much fun!"

They both get their mochi, and take a big bite!
It's super soft and yummy, and not too sweet, just right!

"Susie before we go, I got you a surprise,"
Susie puts out her hands and closes her eyes.

When she opens her eyes she giggles with glee.
"Oh my gosh, James is this origami I see?"

"Yes it is Susie, and the crane is good luck!"
"Thank you," Susie smiles, "Oops thought it was a duck."

"Now Susie, are you ready? There is one more place to see!"

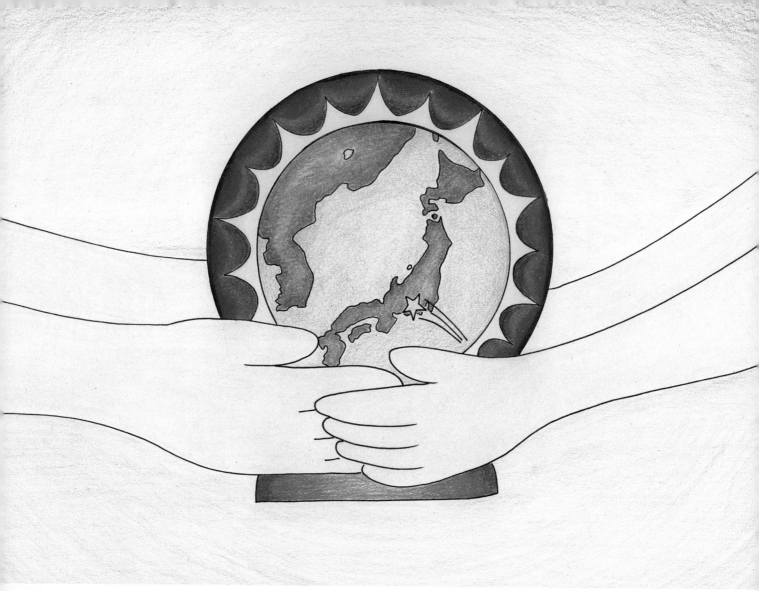

They place their hands on the globe and shout, "Mount Fuji!"

And in the blink of an eye, they are both standing there,
Gazing up at Japan's highest mountain where they both quietly stare.

"Did you know, Susie, Mt. Fuji's an active Volcano?"
"What?" gasps Susie, "Are you crazy? We should go!"

James laughs, "Don't worry, they watch it 24 hours a day,"
"Phew, you should have said that first, you nearly scared me away!"

"It's getting kind of late now, we should make our way back."
They both say, "Home sweet home," and they hear the ground crack!

They both start to fall and tumble through the air!
"Here we go Susie, now we know we're almost there!"

Pa poompf, they both land, into their own bed.
"Hey guys," Dad pops in, "remember what we said?"

James answers, "you told us to be quiet when it's late at night."
"Actually," says Susie, "It's really almost light."

"That is true," Dad agrees, "So let's start the day!"

"Actually," James and Susie ask, "can we sleep in today?"

Map of Japan

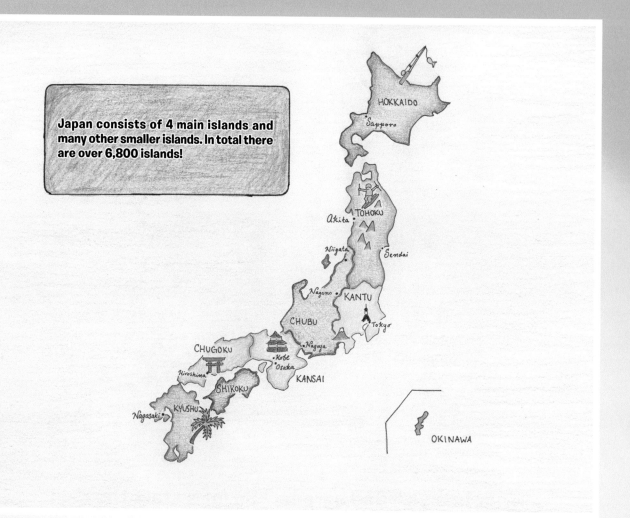

Find out where little James' magic snow globe takes him next!
www.JanineIannelli.com

Follow me on Instagram! @Janineiannelliauthor

Printed in the United States
by Baker & Taylor Publisher Services